This book belongs to:

Dear Albert, Florence and Esme,

I hope you all had a good day at school.

I'm not sure how much you like reading, but I found this great book.

It's about this mouse called George, who has an amazing imagination.

I hope you enjoy it.

Love,

Your Cousin Harry

First published 2016 by Senlac Hill Publishing
Epsom, Surry, United Kingdom
www.SHP.media

Hardback ISBN 978 0 9956897 0 1
Paperback ISBN 978 0 9956897 1 8

For more information on the George the (Almost) Fearless Mouse series of books, visit:
www.FearlessGeorge.SHP.media

Written by Chris Hastings   Illustrated by Kristi Marmor

George

the (almost) fearless mouse

Isn't Afraid of the Dark!

visit www.fearlessgeorge.shp.media for more fun!

Acknowledgements

George would like to squeak a huge thanks to the following for their incredible support

Samuel Guess
Sally Hunter
Stephan Whelan

Miss Lili-mae, Lili-mae's School of Performing Arts
www.lmschoolofperformingarts.co.uk

The team at Treetops Day Nursery and Pre-School
www.treetopsnurseries.co.uk

1066 Productions
www.1066productions.com

FOREWORD

by Dr Elaine Aron

Author of *The Highly Sensitive Child* and *The Highly Sensitive Person*

The story of *George* is a wonderful way to help sensitive children with fears they may have. It is a treasure in this way. But to me it is, above all, about our differences. How do we accept our uniqueness as a sensitive individual, or our differentness from others, especially as we grow older? We may notice that we are different from our brothers and sisters, our classmates, friends, and then work colleagues and partners? How does anyone interpret being different?

Meet *George*. *George* isn't like his brothers and sisters. Why? He has a wonderful strength, fearlessness. Each of us has a special strength and we learn that from *George*. Many sensitive children are cautious because they are reflecting on the world around them, elaborating the possibilities just as adults formulate hypotheses. But hypotheses mean imagining what things may be like, and imagination can be fun, but not always a picture of how things really are. We have to check out the facts. *George* does this for his brothers and sisters, which in turn is role modeling how a sensitive child might check out the facts in order to get over fears.

Parents reading *George* to a sensitive child will want to explore how she or he is the same as and/or different from *George;* looking for a child's particular strength is equivalent to *George*'s fearlessness. This leads into the strength of *George* being so sensitive. Even a sensitive child can be different from other sensitive children. How is this child's sensitivity expressed? Every sensitive child will be a little different from *George*. *George* is not nimble, but many sensitive children have agility as their main strength or excel at team sports by using their sensitivity to anticipate the next move. *George* is not talkative. He is like the majority of HSPs, who are more introverted. But some sensitive children are very talkative, especially at home.

What *George* and other sensitive children will usually have in common is their empathy for others, in this case *George*'s gentle kindness towards Marlon, Monty, and Milo. They often have in common a tendency to notice subtleties and to reflect deeply. The result is that they have helpful insights or intuitions, like *George*, and maybe a lovely, quirky sense of humor. By highlighting how they may differ or be the same as *George*, parents can help children come away from the book not only being less afraid of the dark, but confident that however they are like or not like *George* they might be like him at a deep level.

I hope you are delighted by meeting *George*, I know I was.

To Seraphina, my incredible HSC.
Together and apart, I'll always be there to shine a light into the darkness. Always.

Unless there are spiders. In which case, please call mummy.

An astonishing 1 in 5 of all children is a Highly Sensitive Child (HSC), yet high sensitivity is still largely unrecognised.

HSCs are much more likely to become shy, anxious or depressed and the mishandling and misunderstanding of high sensitivity during childhood frequently causes anxiety and distress and can lead to emotional problems later in life.

To find out if your child is one of the 1 in 5 and for further guidance go to:
www.fearlessgeorge.shp.media/test

George the Mouse was different from other mice.

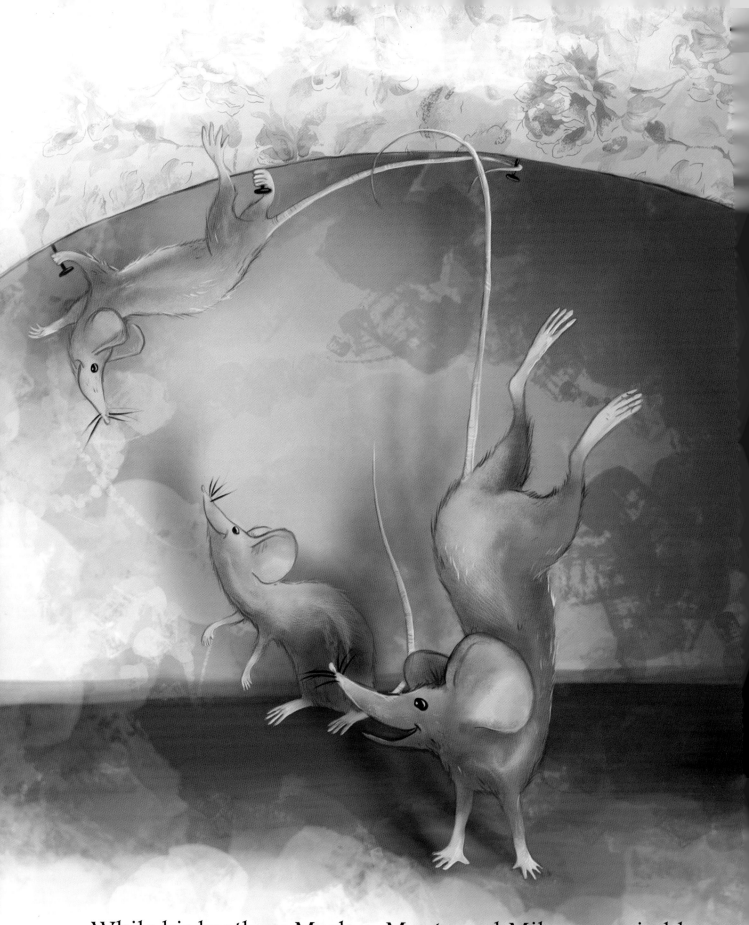

While his brothers Marlon, Monty and Milo were nimble and lightning fast, George was prone to tripping over his tiny pink feet.

While his sisters Milly, Molly and Mabel were talkative and loud, George was a thoughtful mouse of few squeaks.

But what truly set him apart, was that despite being the smallest, quietest, gentlest mouse you could ever possibly meet...

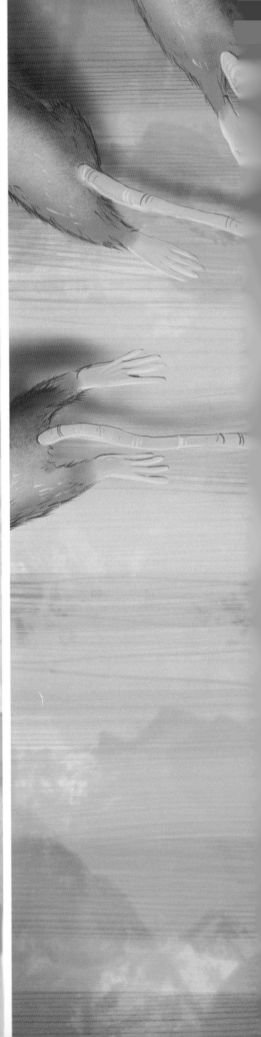

...he was also the most fearless.

In truth, George wasn't afraid of anything.

Well, almost anything.

Every evening, Mama Mouse would tuck them into bed, pulling the covers up to their tiny pink noses; and as the lights went out, all the mice would tremble nervously in the gloom.

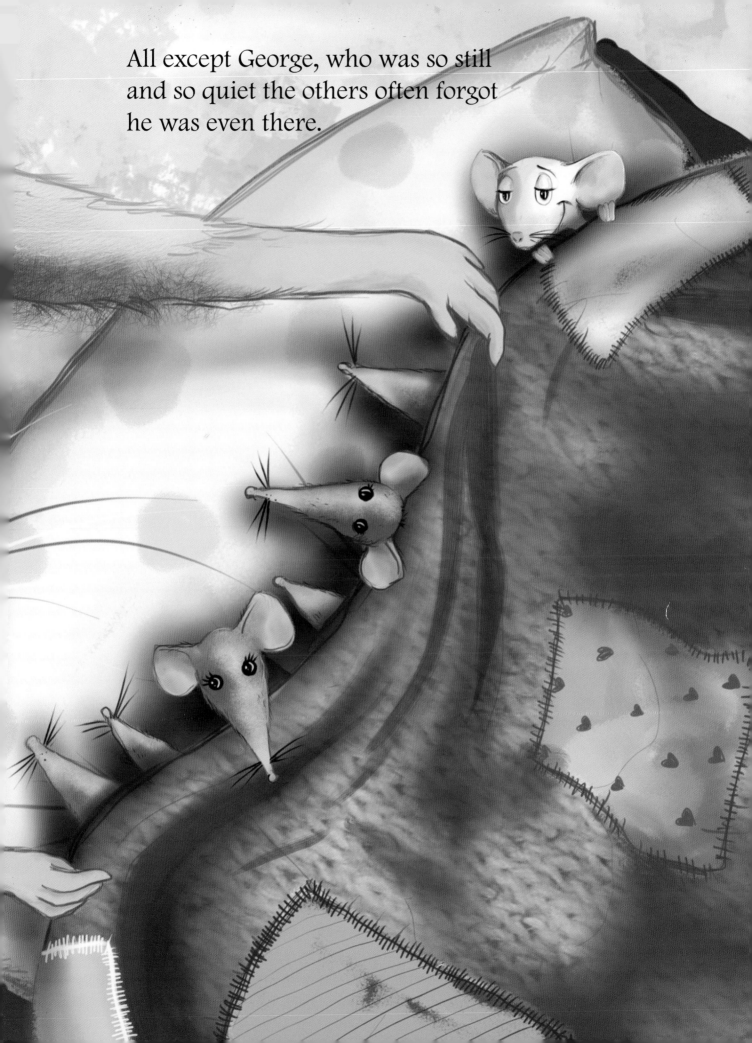

All except George, who was so still
and so quiet the others often forgot
he was even there.

One star-speckled night, Monty turned to George and squeaked
"I guess you think we're silly, being afraid of the dark."

But George didn't think it was silly. Not silly at all. And he wrapped a protective arm around his brother as they all drifted off to sleep.

The next day, George passed a dense, dark forest, thick with whispering trees and thought about Marlon, Monty and Milo.

He passed an unlit room that danced with dark shadows and thought about Milly, Molly and Mabel.

And as the day drained away and the sky grew purple, he thought about them all.

That night, when they were in bed and George felt the covers quiver and shake, he took a long, deep breath.

"When they're small," he said, "everyone is afraid of the dark. The littlest ant to the biggest roaringest lion. Mama Mouse. Even Papa Mouse. And it's not silly. But it is funny."

"Because, there's really nothing there," George grinned.

He switched on the light and showed them the books behind the curtains, the toys under the bed, the clothes in the wardrobe.

And he was absolutely right. There were no monsters and nothing to be afraid of. Just books, toys and clothes.

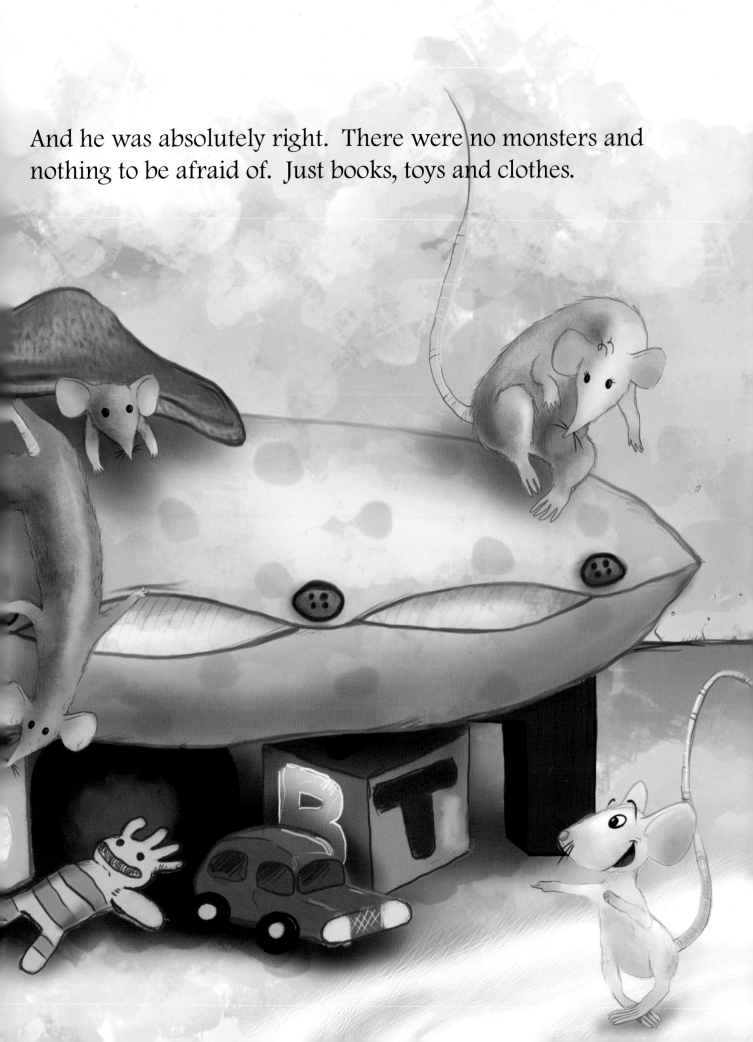

"There's no such thing as monsters, but your imagination is an incredible thing. You use it to create words and songs; to pretend to be dinosaurs and fairies."

"Imagination is like a crayon and the dark is a piece of paper. Our imagination paints pictures in the dark just like when we draw."

"Like when you look at a cloud in the sky and see a kitten or candy floss," squeaked Monty.

"Exactly," George replied. "It's not real. It's just pretend.
So you can make-believe it's anything you want."

"Anything?" squeaked Milo.

And with that, Milo peered into the gloom of a far corner, where the moon just broke through the curtains, and he smiled a big smile.

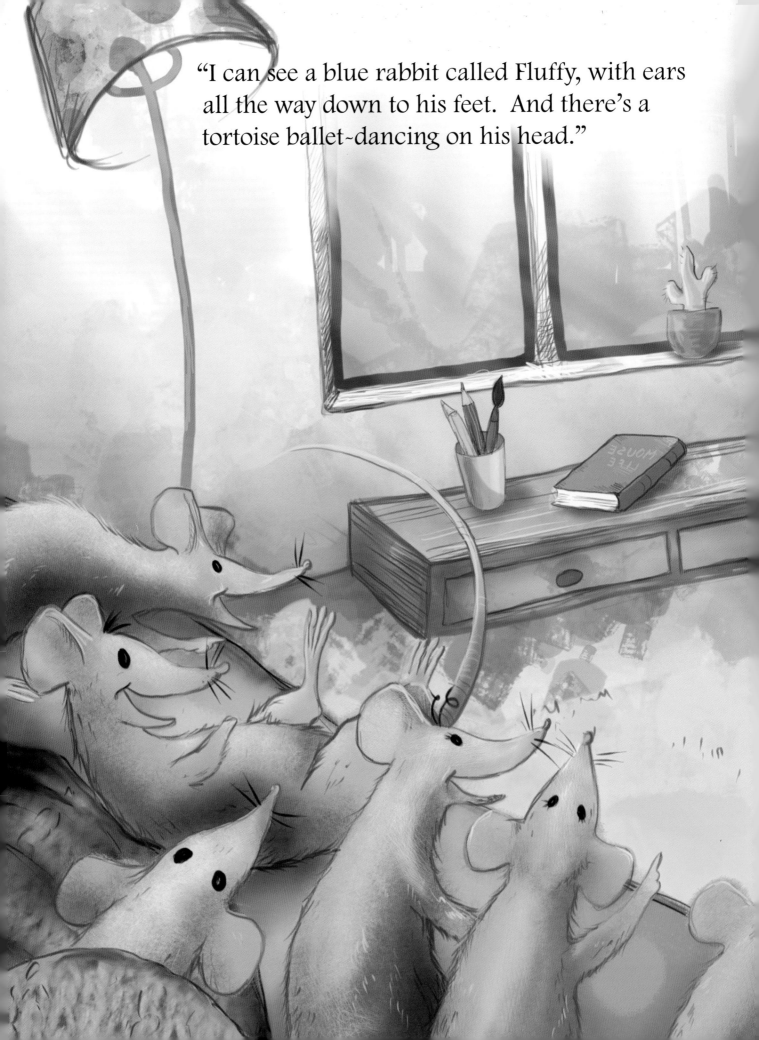

"I can see a blue rabbit called Fluffy, with ears all the way down to his feet. And there's a tortoise ballet-dancing on his head."

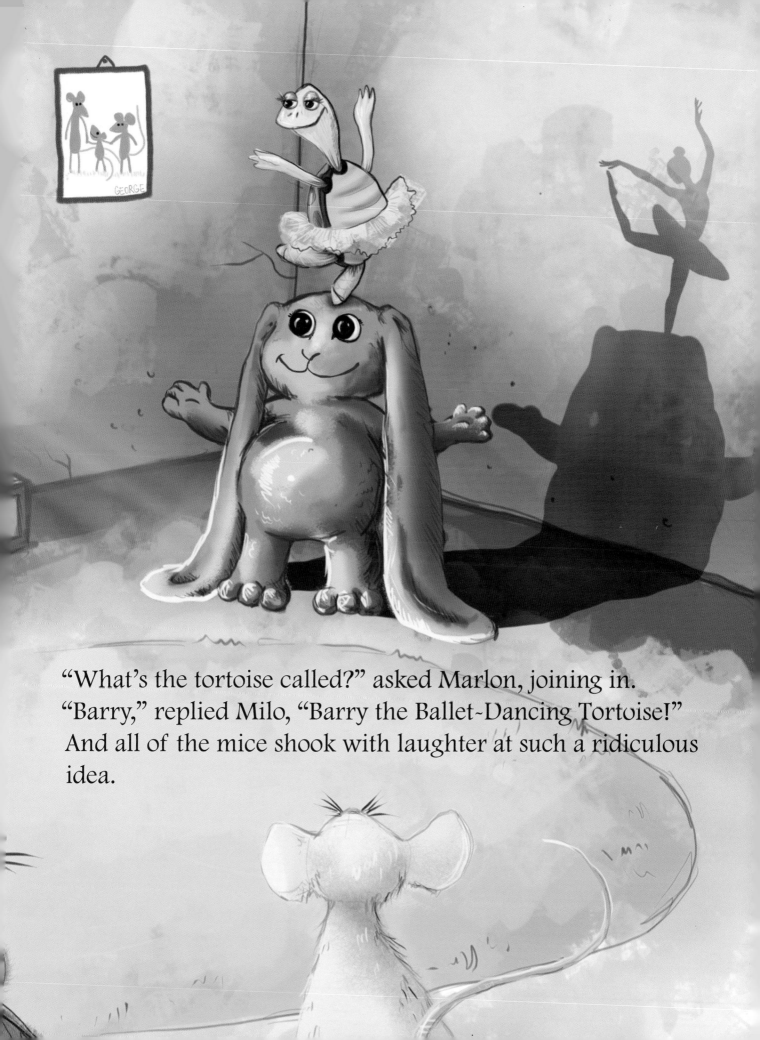

"What's the tortoise called?" asked Marlon, joining in.
"Barry," replied Milo, "Barry the Ballet-Dancing Tortoise!"
And all of the mice shook with laughter at such a ridiculous
idea.

Molly, who had been listening and felt a lot better now, said to George "Isn't there anything you're afraid of?"

George thought for a while. "Only one thing," he replied.
'Being different."

"But you are
different,"
said Molly.
"Marvellously
different!"

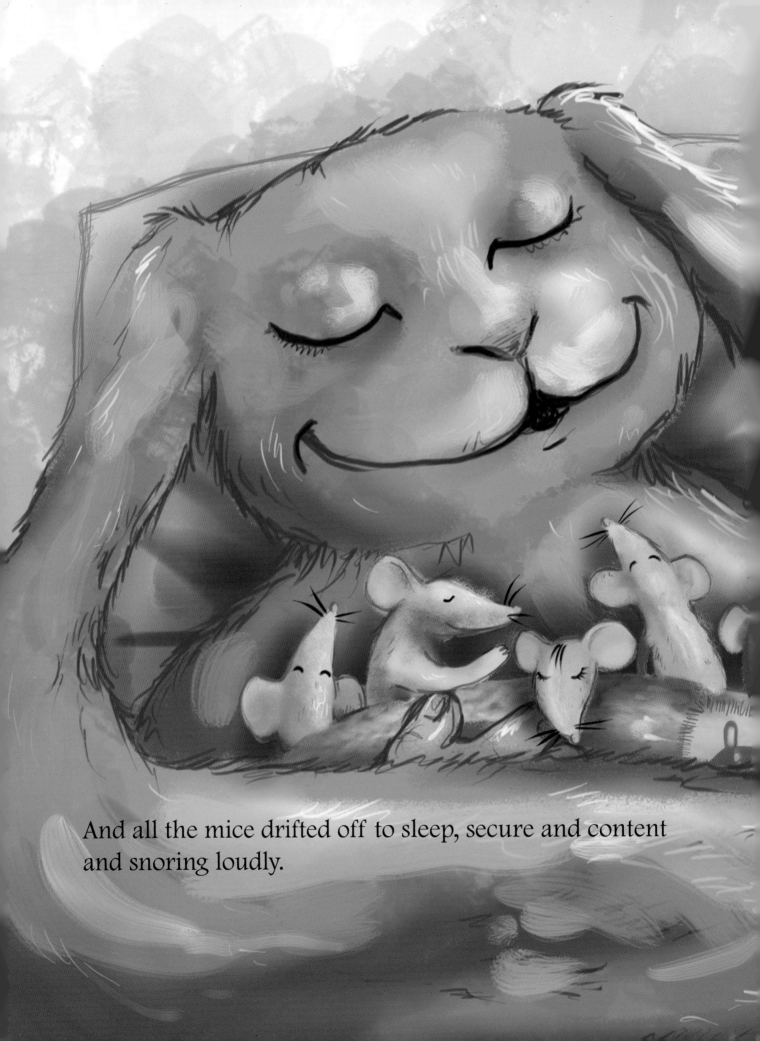

And all the mice drifted off to sleep, secure and content and snoring loudly.

Even George, who, as you know, was marvellously different from other mice.

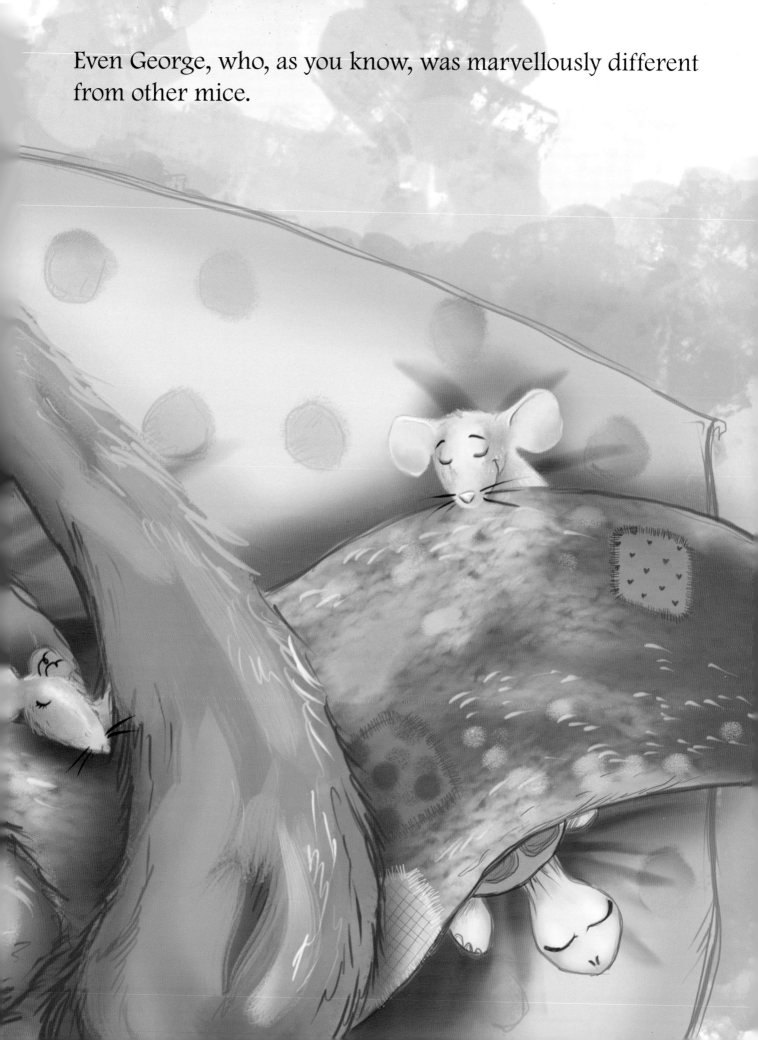